CLASSICS ILLUSTRATED™

presents

KIDNAPPED

by Robert Louis Stevenson

CCS Books

Also available from CCS Books

NICHOLAS NICKLEBY
ROBINSON CRUSOE
WUTHERING HEIGHTS
JANE EYRE
TREASURE ISLAND
ROBIN HOOD
LES MISÉRABLES
THE JUNGLE BOOK
A CHRISTMAS CAROL
THE LAST DAYS OF POMPEII
THE HUNCHBACK OF NOTRE DAME
AROUND THE WORLD IN 80 DAYS

For a full list of titles, go to www.ccsbooks.com

CLASSICS ILLUSTRATED: KIDNAPPED
ISBN: 9781911238225

Published by CCS Books
A trading name of Classic Comic Store Ltd.
Unit B, Castle Industrial Park, Pear Tree Lane, Newbury, Berkshire, RG14 2EZ, UK

Email: enquiries@ccsbooks.com
Tel: UK 01635 30890

First CCS Books edition: October 2017

Painted cover: Unknown
Illustrated by: Robert H. Webb
Adaptation: John O'Rourke
Re-origination: Christina Choma, Eva Oja and Jaak Jarve
New cover design: Ray Lipscombe
Additional material: Jay Hoffman, Jeff Brooks and Jon Brooks

Printed in China

KIDNAPPED

by Robert Louis Stevenson

DURING THE EARLY PERIOD OF MARITIME SERVICE, MEN, YOUNG AND OLD, WERE SHANGHAIED INTO VIRTUAL SLAVERY AT THE HANDS OF UNSCRUPULOUS GANGS. THESE MEN WERE OFTEN BEATEN OR DRUGGED INTO SUBMISSION AND THEN TURNED OVER TO CRUEL AND SEEMINGLY HEARTLESS SHIP OWNERS AND THEIR CAPTAINS FOR HANDSOME REWARDS.

THIS IS THE STORY OF A YOUNG MAN WHO WAS IMPRESSED INTO A SHIP'S CREW AND HIS DETERMINED FIGHT TO REGAIN HIS RIGHTFUL PLACE IN THE WORLD.

AT HIS FATHER'S DEATH IN THE SUMMER OF 1751, DAVID BALFOUR LEFT THE VILLAGE OF ESSENDEAN, SCOTLAND...

AND ALONG THE WAY HE WAS MET BY MR CAMPBELL, THE VILLAGE MINISTER...

YOUR FATHER GAVE ME IN CHARGE A CERTAIN LETTER WHICH HE SAID WAS YOUR INHERITANCE.

THANK YOU, SIR.

To the hands of Ebenezer Balfour, Esq. of Shaws, these in his house of Shaws, will be delivered by my son, David Balfour

THE HOUSE OF SHAWS! WHAT HAD MY POOR FATHER TO DO WITH THE HOUSE OF SHAWS?

NAY, WHO CAN TELL THAT? THE NAME OF THAT FAMILY, DAVIE BOY, IS THE NAME YOU BEAR... BALFOUR OF SHAWS...

MR CAMPBELL, IF YOU WERE IN MY SHOES, WOULD YOU GO?

OF A SURETY, THAT WOULD I, AND WITHOUT PAUSE.

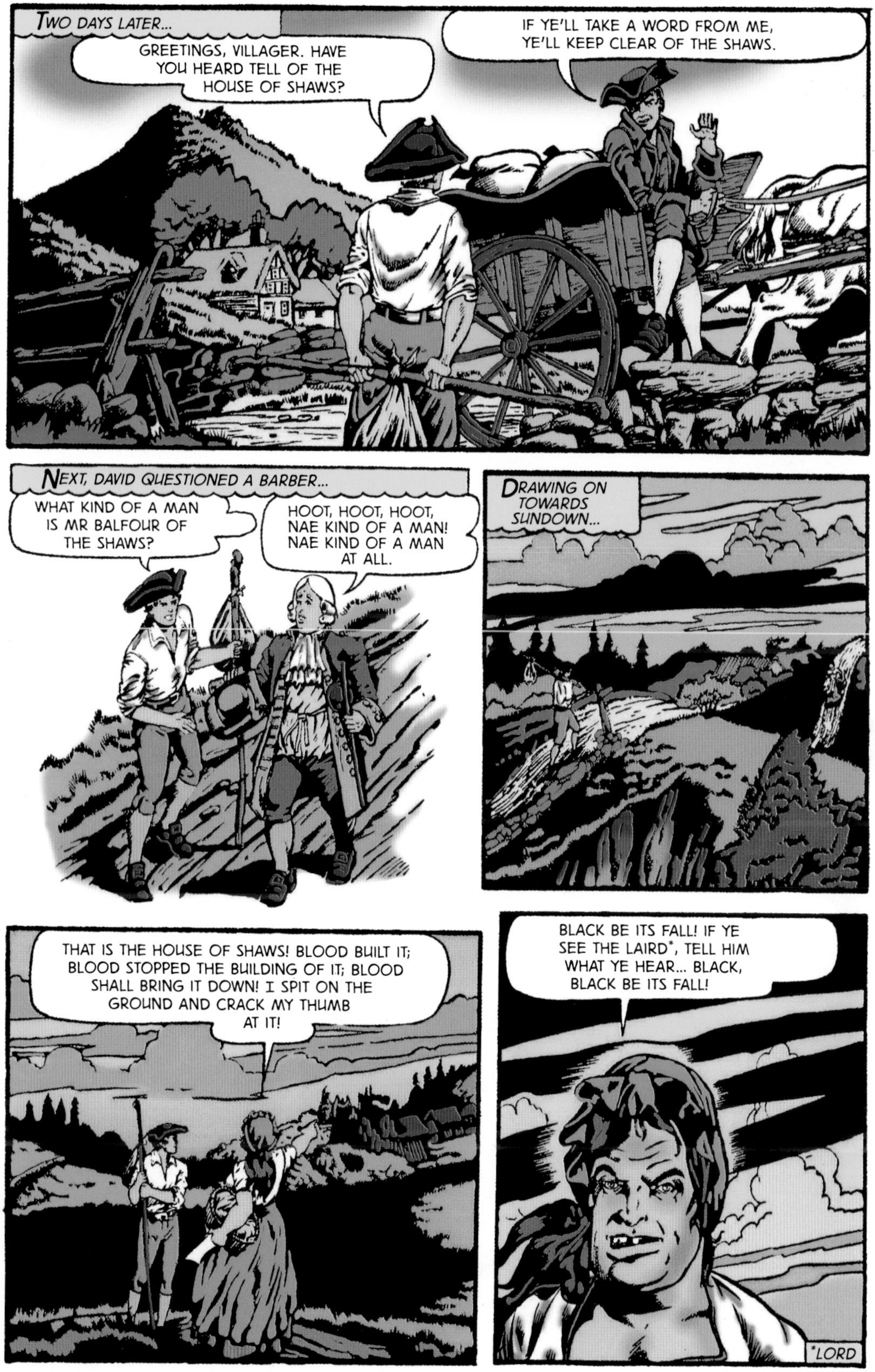
TWO DAYS LATER...
GREETINGS, VILLAGER. HAVE YOU HEARD TELL OF THE HOUSE OF SHAWS?
IF YE'LL TAKE A WORD FROM ME, YE'LL KEEP CLEAR OF THE SHAWS.
NEXT, DAVID QUESTIONED A BARBER...
WHAT KIND OF A MAN IS MR BALFOUR OF THE SHAWS?
HOOT, HOOT, HOOT, NAE KIND OF A MAN! NAE KIND OF A MAN AT ALL.
DRAWING ON TOWARDS SUNDOWN...
THAT IS THE HOUSE OF SHAWS! BLOOD BUILT IT; BLOOD STOPPED THE BUILDING OF IT; BLOOD SHALL BRING IT DOWN! I SPIT ON THE GROUND AND CRACK MY THUMB AT IT!
BLACK BE ITS FALL! IF YE SEE THE LAIRD*, TELL HIM WHAT YE HEAR... BLACK, BLACK BE ITS FALL!
*LORD

DAVID FINALLY ARRIVED AT THE HOUSE OF SHAWS, BUT HIS KNOCKING WAS GREETED WITH DEAD SILENCE...

THEN, QUITE SUDDENLY, A FIGURE APPEARED AT THE WINDOW... STARTLED BUT DETERMINED, DAVID GATHERED HIS VOICE...

I HAVE COME HERE WITH A LETTER TO MR EBENEZER BALFOUR OF THE SHAWS. IS - IS HE HERE?

YE CAN PUT IT DOWN UPON THE DOORSTEP, AND BE OFF WITH YE!

I WILL DO NO SUCH THING. I WILL DELIVER IT INTO MR BALFOUR'S HANDS AS IT WAS MEANT I SHOULD DO. IT IS A LETTER OF INTRODUCTION.

WHO ARE YE?

THEY CALL ME DAVID BALFOUR.

IS YOUR FATHER DEAD? AY, HE'LL BE DEAD AND THAT'LL BE WHAT BRINGS YOU TO MY DOOR. WELL, MAN, I'LL LET YOU IN.

GO INTO THE KITCHEN AND TOUCH NAETHING!

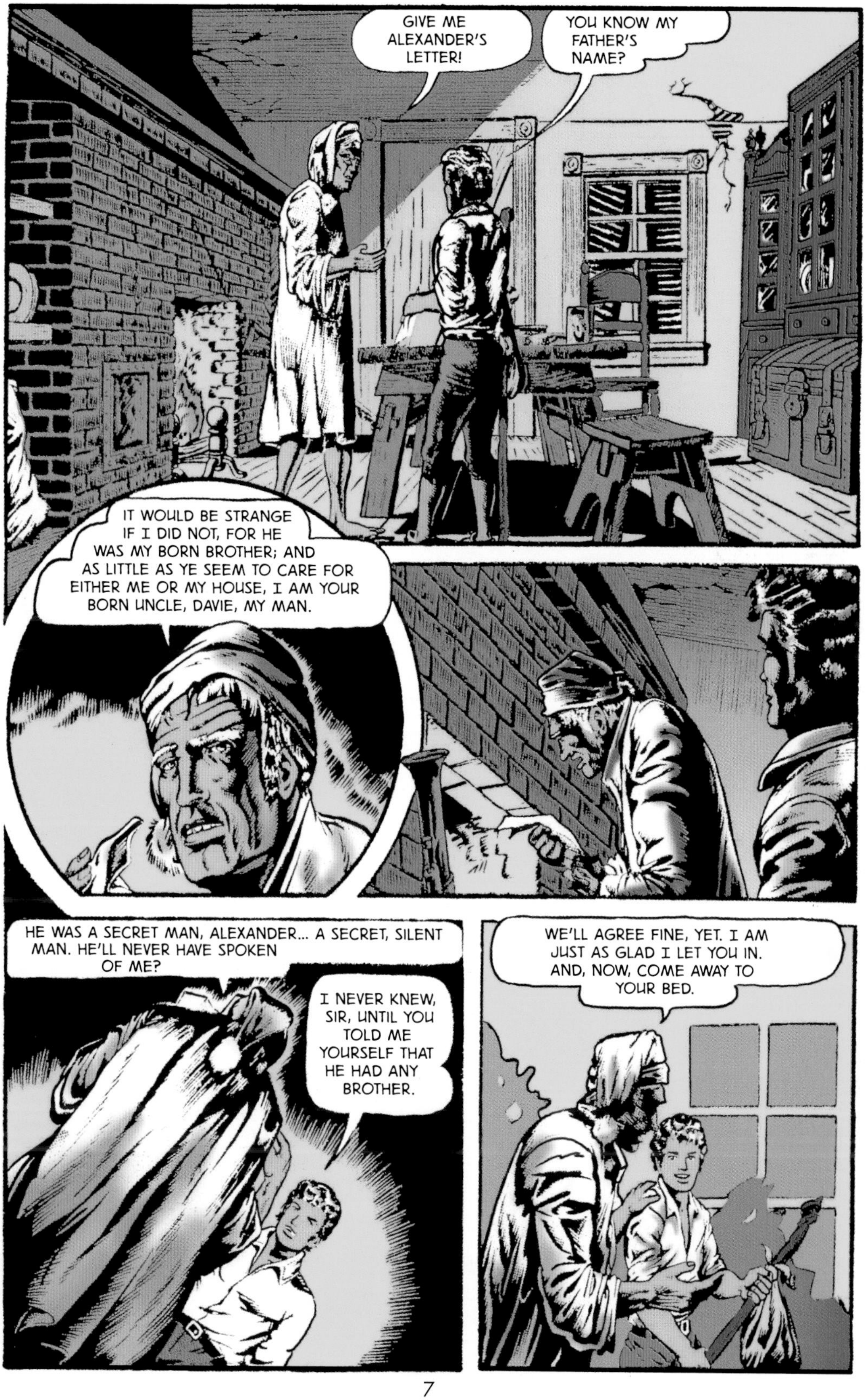
GIVE ME ALEXANDER'S LETTER!
YOU KNOW MY FATHER'S NAME?
IT WOULD BE STRANGE IF I DID NOT, FOR HE WAS MY BORN BROTHER; AND AS LITTLE AS YE SEEM TO CARE FOR EITHER ME OR MY HOUSE, I AM YOUR BORN UNCLE, DAVIE, MY MAN.
HE WAS A SECRET MAN, ALEXANDER... A SECRET, SILENT MAN. HE'LL NEVER HAVE SPOKEN OF ME?
I NEVER KNEW, SIR, UNTIL YOU TOLD ME YOURSELF THAT HE HAD ANY BROTHER.
WE'LL AGREE FINE, YET. I AM JUST AS GLAD I LET YOU IN. AND, NOW, COME AWAY TO YOUR BED.

WHILE BEING LED TO HIS ROOM IN DARKNESS, DAVID BECAME AWARE OF HIS UNCLE'S MISERLY WAYS...

HOOT-TOOT, THERE'S A FINE MOON!

NEITHER MOON NOR STAR, SIR, DARK AS A PIT!

AND BEFORE HE COULD PROTEST, THE DOOR WAS LOCKED...

LIGHTS IN A HOUSE IS A THING I DO NOT AGREE WITH. I AM FEARED OF FIRES. GOOD NIGHT TO YE.

THE NEXT MORN...

UNCLE EBENEZER!

DAVID HURRIED THROUGH A MEAGRE BREAKFAST...

DAVIE, I MEAN TO DO RIGHT BY YOU, BUT WHILE I AM TAKING A BIT THINK TO MYSELF OF WHAT'S THE BEST THING TO PUT YOU TO - NO LETTERS, NO MESSAGES, NO KIND OF WORD TO ANYBODY OR ELSE, THERE'S MY DOOR!

I'VE NO REASON TO SUPPOSE YOU MEAN ANYTHING BUT WELL BY ME. FOR ALL THAT, IF YOU SHOW ME YOUR DOOR AGAIN, I'LL TAKE YOU AT YOUR WORD.

NO, NO, I DIDN'T MEAN THAT. WHAT'S MINE IS YOURS, DAVIE, MY MAN, AND WHAT'S YOURS IS MINE.

SEEKING ENTERTAINMENT, DAVID CAME UPON A STRANGE INSCRIPTION SCRATCHED ACROSS THE FLY-LEAF OF A BOOK...

To my brother Ebenezer on his fifth Birthday Alexander

IF MY FATHER WAS THE YOUNGER BROTHER, HE MUST HAVE MADE AN ERROR. OR HE MUST HAVE WRITTEN BEFORE HE WAS YET FIVE – IN AN EXCELLENT, MANLY HAND.

UNCLE, WAS MY FATHER QUICK AT HIS BOOK AS A LAD?

ALEXANDER? NO' HIM! I WAS FAR QUICKER MYSELF. I COULD READ AS SOON AS HE COULD.

SUDDENLY...

WHAT MAKES YE ASK THAT?

TAKE YOUR HAND FROM MY JACKET!

YE SHOULD NOT SPEAK TO ME ABOUT YOUR FATHER, DAVID. HE WAS ALL THE BROTHER THAT I EVER HAD.

EBENEZER PLEADED FOR UNDERSTANDING... BUT DAVID DETECTED A FEAR OF HIMSELF IN HIS UNCLE'S ACTIONS...

NOT ANOTHER WORD PASSED BETWEEN THE TWO THROUGHOUT THE ENTIRE DAY. LIKE CAT AND MOUSE, THEY SAT DOWN TO THEIR EVENING MEAL, EACH STEALTHILY OBSERVING THE OTHER. FINALLY, EBENEZER BROKE THE SILENCE...

DAVID, I'VE BEEN THINKING... THERE'S A WEE BIT OF MONEY I HALF PROMISED YE BEFORE YE WERE BORN. I PROMISED IT TO YOUR FATHER.

A LIE!

FORTY POUNDS!* AND IF YE'LL STEP OUT BY THE DOOR A MINUTE, I'LL GET IT AND CALL YOU IN AGAIN.

*A POUND IS WORTH APPROX. £200 TODAY.

A STORM COMING UP...

SOON, DAVID WAS CALLED IN AGAIN...

THAT'LL SHOW YOU! I'M A QUEER MAN AND STRANGE WI' STRANGERS; BUT MY WORD IS MY BOND AND THERE'S PROOF OF IT.

AND BY COUNT... FORTY POUNDS.

DAVID'S SUSPICIONS WERE NOT DISPELLED BY HIS UNCLE'S GIFT. HE WONDERED WHAT WOULD COME NEXT...

I WANT NO THANKS. IT'S A PLEASURE TO ME TO DO RIGHT BY MY BROTHER'S SON. AND SEE HERE, IT'S TIT FOR TAT.

I AM READY TO PROVE MY GRATITUDE IN ANY REASONABLE DEGREE, UNCLE EBENEZER.

WELL, LET'S BEGIN. HERE'S THE KEY TO THE STAIR-TOWER AT THE FAR END OF THE HOUSE. YE CAN ONLY WIN INTO IT FROM THE OUTSIDE, FOR THAT PART OF THE HOUSE IS NOT FINISHED. BRING DOWN THE CHEST AT THE TOP.

CAN I HAVE A LIGHT, SIR?

NO, NO LIGHTS IN MY HOUSE.

ARE THE STAIRS GOOD?

THEY'RE GRAND. KEEP TO THE WALL, THERE'S NO BANISTERS!

DAVID HURRIED TO FINISH HIS TASK BEFORE THE STORM BROKE...

HMMM...

11

A FLASH OF JAGGED LIGHTNING LIT THE ENTRANCE FOR A SPLIT SECOND...

AH, THERE'S THE STAIRCASE.

IN THE BLACKNESS, DAVID PRESSED CLOSE TO THE HEWN STONE WALL AND WITH A QUICK BEATING HEART RECALLED HIS UNCLE'S WARNING...

THERE'S NO BANISTER... KEEP TO THE WALL...

STRANGE... SEEMS TO GROW AIRIER... THERE'S A LITTLE MORE LIGHT AHEAD...

THEN, ONCE MORE, THE LIGHTNING FLASHED... AND THE TRUTH OF HIS MISSION WAS PLAINLY REVEALED...

ONE MORE STEP WOULD HAVE SENT ME CRASHING TO... TO... MY UNCLE SENT ME HERE TO DIE!

YES, DAVID'S UNCLE HAD SENT DAVID TO DIE... BUT HIS PLAN WAS THWARTED BY A SINGLE STEP...

ANGRY COURAGE FILLED DAVID'S HEART AS HE SANK TO HIS KNEES AND SLOWLY... SLOWLY ASCENDED, FEELING OUT EVERY INCH BEFORE HIM...

IN TOTAL DARKNESS, HE REACHED ANOTHER TURN IN THE STAIRCASE... HIS HAND REACHED OUT BEFORE HIM AND THERE WAS NOTHING BEYOND... THE STAIRS HAD BEEN CARRIED NO HIGHER...

FINALLY, HE REACHED THE GROUND... AND THERE, SILHOUETTED AGAINST THE KITCHEN DOORWAY...

HE'S WAITING! WAITING FOR THE SOUND OF MY FALL!

MIDST THE CRASH OF A CLAP OF THUNDER, EBENEZER DASHED INTO HIS HOUSE IN PANIC, AS IF HE HAD HEARD THE ALMIGHTY'S VOICE DENOUNCING MURDER OR THE THUD OF DAVID'S FALL...

WITH TREMBLING FINGERS, HE REACHED FOR HIS BRANDY, WHILE, UNHEARD, DAVID ENTERED...

AND DAVID PREPARED A SURPRISE...

EBENEZER SWOONED IN A DEAD FAINT, BUT DAVID LOST NO TIME. SNATCHING HIS UNCLE'S KEYS, HE RUSHED TO THE CUPBOARD, SEEKING ARMS AGAINST FURTHER EVIL...

THIS DIRK* MAY BECOME A DEAR FRIEND TO ME...

*DAGGER

14

DAVID THEN REVIVED HIS SCHEMING UNCLE...

ARE... ARE YE ALIVE?

THAT I AM, SMALL THANKS TO YOU!

WHY DID YOU TRY TO KILL ME?

I'LL TELL YE IN THE MORN, AS SURE AS DEATH I WILL.

BECAUSE OF HIS UNCLE'S WEAKNESS FROM FRIGHT, DAVID AGREED TO WAIT TILL MORNING FOR AN EXPLANATION AND LOCKED EBENEZER IN HIS ROOM FOR THE NIGHT...

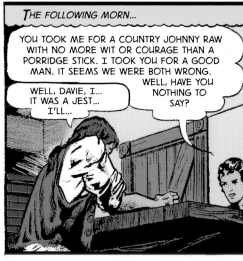

THE FOLLOWING MORN...

YOU TOOK ME FOR A COUNTRY JOHNNY RAW WITH NO MORE WIT OR COURAGE THAN A PORRIDGE STICK. I TOOK YOU FOR A GOOD MAN. IT SEEMS WE WERE BOTH WRONG.

WELL, DAVIE, I... IT WAS A JEST... I'LL...

WELL, HAVE YOU NOTHING TO SAY?

A KNOCKING AT THE DOOR INTERRUPTED THEM...

SIT WHERE YOU ARE!

WHAT CHEER, MATE? I'VE BROUGHT A LETTER FROM OLD HEASYOASY TO MR BELFLOWER.

COME IN TO THE HOUSE.

HMMM... GOOD PORRIDGE...

READ THAT!

The Hawes Inn at the Queen's Ferry

Sir: I lie here with my hawser up and down and send my cabin boy to inform. If you have any further commands for overseas, today will be the last occasion.

your humble servant,

Elias Hoseason

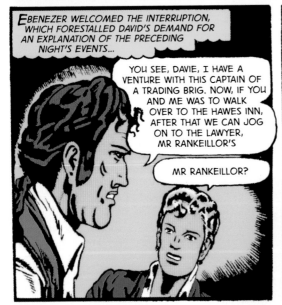

EBENEZER WELCOMED THE INTERRUPTION, WHICH FORESTALLED DAVID'S DEMAND FOR AN EXPLANATION OF THE PRECEDING NIGHT'S EVENTS...

YOU SEE, DAVIE, I HAVE A VENTURE WITH THIS CAPTAIN OF A TRADING BRIG. NOW, IF YOU AND ME WAS TO WALK OVER TO THE HAWES INN, AFTER THAT WE CAN JOG ON TO THE LAWYER, MR RANKEILLOR'S

MR RANKEILLOR?

DAVID HEARD THAT MR RANKEILLOR WOULD BE HIS UNCLE'S WITNESS TO THE FACT THAT HE MEANT DAVID NO HARM.

YE BE UNWILLING TO BELIEVE MY NAKED WORD, BUT YE'LL BELIEVE RANKEILLOR. HE'S HIGHLY RESPECTED AND HE KNEW YOUR FATHER.

VERY WELL. LET US GO TO THE FERRY.

DAVID JUDGED FROM THE CABIN BOY'S DESCRIPTION THAT THE BRIG, "COVENANT", AS SHE WAS SO PIOUSLY CALLED, WAS RATHER A CURSE UPON THE SEAS...

WHY, THEN, DON'T YOU FIND A REPUTABLE LIFE ON SHORE?

OH, THERE'S WORSE OFF THAN ME. THERE'S THE TWENTY POUNDERS.*

*CRIMINALS WHO WERE SENT OVERSEAS TO SLAVERY IN NORTH AMERICA.

I'M GLAD YE ARE HERE IN TIME, MR BALFOUR. THE WIND'S FAIR AND THE TIDE UPON THE TURN. WE WILL SEE THE OLD COAL BUCKET ON THE ISLE OF MAY TONIGHT.

CAPTAIN, YOU KEEP YOUR ROOM UNCOMFORTABLY HOT.

DAVID ALSO FOUND THE ROOM TOO HOT AND TOOK ADVANTAGE OF AN EXCUSE TO RUN DOWNSTAIRS...

THE CREW OF THE BRIG, "COVENANT".

COME ABOARD MY BRIG FOR HALF AN HOUR TILL THE SUN SETS, AND DRINK A BOWL WITH ME.

MY UNCLE AND I HAVE AN APPOINTMENT WITH A LAWYER.

THE CAPTAIN PROMISED THAT THE BRIG WOULD SET DAVID AND HIS UNCLE ASHORE AT THE TOWN PIER CLOSE TO LAWYER RANKEILLOR'S HOUSE... THEN, LOWERING HIS VOICE, HE WHISPERED TO DAVID...

TAKE CARE OF THAT OLD FOX. HE MEANS MISCHIEF. COME ABOARD TILL I CAN GET A WORD WITH YE.

DAVID WAS PERSUADED TO VISIT THE "COVENANT" WITH HIS UNCLE...

ABOARD THE BRIG, CAPTAIN HOSEASON SHOWED DAVID THE SIGHTS... SUDDENLY, DAVID MISSED HIS UNCLE... HE RUSHED TO THE BULWARKS...

HELP! HELP! MURDER!

QUIET, YOU!

DAVID WAS CARRIED BELOW WHERE HE REMAINED SEVERAL DAYS. LATER, THE LIMP BODY OF RANSOME, THE CABIN BOY, WAS BROUGHT BELOW.

WE WANT YE TO SERVE IN THE ROUND-HOUSE, DAVID, YE'LL CHANGE BERTHS WITH RANSOME.

AS THE "COVENANT" SHEERED SWIFTLY ALONG ITS COURSE, THE BODY OF THE DEAD CABIN BOY, RANSOME, WAS SLIPPED SILENTLY INTO THE SEA.

WELL, HE BROUGHT ME A DIRTY PANNIKIN.*

SIT DOWN, MR SHUAN, YE SOT! SWINE! DO YE KNOW WHAT YE'VE DONE? YE'VE MURDERED THE BOY!

CAPT'N, YE SHOULD HAVE INTERFERED LONG AGO. IT'S TOO LATE NOW.

*TIN CUP

MR RIACH, THIS NIGHT'S WORK MUST NEVER BE KNOWN IN DYSART. THE BOY WENT OVERBOARD, SIR. THAT'S WHAT THE STORY IS!

BAD WEATHER FOLLOWED THE "COVENANT". SOME DAYS, SHE MADE A LITTLE WAY; OTHERS, SHE WAS ACTUALLY DRIVEN BACK. ON THE TENTH DAY, A THICK WHITE FOG HID ONE END OF THE BRIG FROM THE OTHER...

WITHOUT WARNING, THE "COVENANT" SUDDENLY CRASHED...

SHE'S STRUCK!

NO, MR RIACH, WE'VE RUN A BOAT DOWN!

THE CAPTAIN WAS RIGHT. THE "COVENANT" HAD RAMMED AND SUNK A BOAT IN THE FOG. OF ALL THE PASSENGERS AND CREW, THERE WAS ONLY ONE SURVIVOR...

I AM VEXED ABOUT THE BOAT, SIR.

THERE ARE SOME GOOD MEN GONE TO THE BOTTOM THAT I WOULD RATHER SEE ON THE DRY LAND AGAIN THAN HALF A SCORE OF BOATS.

TO BE QUITE PLAIN WITH YE, IF I GOT INTO THE HANDS OF THE RED-COATED GENTRY, IT IS LIKE IT WOULD GO HARD WITH ME. IF YE CAN SET ME ASHORE WHERE I WAS GOING, I HAVE THAT UPON ME WHICH WILL REWARD YOU HIGHLY FOR YOUR TROUBLE.

IN FRANCE? NO, SIR, THAT I CANNAE DO. BUT WHERE YE COME FROM, WE MIGHT TALK OF THAT.

HALF OF THE GOLD IN YOUR BELT AND I'M YOUR MAN.

SIR, NOT A PENNY OF IT BELONGS TO ME, BUT I WILL GIVE YOU SIXTY GUINEAS IF YE SET ME ON THE LINNHE LOCH.*

**A FJORD IN WESTERN SCOTLAND*

WELL, WHAT MUST BE MUST! SIXTY GUINEAS* **AND DONE! HERE'S MY HAND UPON IT!**

AND HERE'S MINE!

**A GUINEA IS WORTH APPROX. £215 TODAY*

DAVID REGARDED THE STRANGER WITH GREAT INTEREST. AN EXILE AND A REBEL, HE HAD COME FROM THE HIGHLANDS AT THE RISK OF HIS LIFE TO COLLECT MONEY FOR HIS CHIEF WHO HAD TAKEN SERVICE WITH THE FRENCH.

SO YOU'RE A JACOBITE?

AYE, AND YOU, BY YOUR LONG FACE, SHOULD BE A WHIG!

BETWIXT AND BETWEEN!

AND THAT IS NOTHING. BUT I'M SAYING, MR BETWIXT AND BETWEEN, THIS BOTTLE IS DRY. IT'S HARD FOR ME TO PAY SIXTY GUINEAS AND BE GRUDGED A DRAM* UPON THE BACK OF IT!

I'LL SEE WHAT I CAN DO ABOUT THAT.

...AND THE LAD OVERHEARD A PLOT...

COULDN'T WE WILE HIM OUT OF THE ROUND-HOUSE?

HE'S BETTER WHERE HE IS. HE HASN'T ROOM TO USE HIS SWORD. WE CAN GET THE MAN IN TALK, ONE UPON EACH SIDE AND PIN HIM UP BY THE TWO ARMS.

AT THE SIGHT OF DAVID, THERE WAS A SUDDEN SILENCE, THEN...

CAPTAIN, THE GENTLEMAN IS SEEKING A DRAM* AND THE BOTTLE'S OUT. WILL YOU GIVE ME THE KEY?

HERE'S OUR CHANCE TO GET THE FIREARMS. DAVID, DO YOU KNOW WHERE THE PISTOLS ARE?

AYE, DAVID KNOWS. YE SEE, DAVID, YON WILD HIELANDMAN IS A DANGER TO THE SHIP BESIDES BEING A FOE TO KING GEORGE.

*ALCOHOLIC DRINK

21

PLANNING TO ROB THE STRANGER, THE CAPTAIN EXPLAINED TO DAVID THAT ALL THE FIREARMS AND POWDER WERE IN THE ROUND-HOUSE. NOT WANTING TO AROUSE THE MAN'S SUSPICION, HE ASKED DAVID TO BRING THE PISTOLS SO HE COULD TAKE THE STRANGER BY SURPRISE.

IF YE DO IT CLEVERLY, DAVIE, I'LL BEAR IT IN MY MIND WHEN IT'LL BE GOOD FOR YOU TO HAVE FRIENDS, AN' THAT'LL BE WHEN WE GET TO CAROLINA.

AND SEE HERE, DAVIE, YOUR MAN HAS A BELTFUL OF GOLD. I CAN GIVE YOU MY WORD THAT YOU SHALL HAVE YOUR FINGERS ON IT.

THE FEAR OF DEATH WAS BEFORE DAVID AS HE RETURNED TO THE ROUND-HOUSE. HE HAD CONSENTED TO DO THE CAPTAIN'S BIDDING IN ORDER TO WARN THE STRANGER - BUT WHAT COULD A MAN AND BOY DO, HE WONDERED, AGAINST THE WHOLE SHIP'S COMPANY?

DO YE WANT TO BE KILLED?

QUICKLY, DAVID RELATED THE PLOT TO ROB AND KILL THE MAN...

AYE, AYE, BUT THEY HAVEN'T GOT ME YET. WILL YE STAND WITH ME?

THAT I WILL. I AM NOT A THIEF NOR YET A MURDERER. I'LL STAND BY YOU.

ALAN BRECK THEY CALL ME. WHAT'S YOUR NAME?

DAVID BALFOUR OF SHAWS.

FIRST OF ALL, HOW MANY ARE AGAINST US?

FIFTEEN.

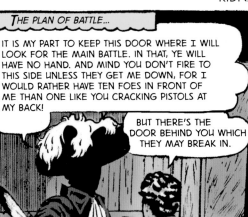

THE PLAN OF BATTLE...

IT IS MY PART TO KEEP THIS DOOR WHERE I WILL LOOK FOR THE MAIN BATTLE. IN THAT, YE WILL HAVE NO HAND. AND MIND YOU DON'T FIRE TO THIS SIDE UNLESS THEY GET ME DOWN, FOR I WOULD RATHER HAVE TEN FOES IN FRONT OF ME THAN ONE LIKE YOU CRACKING PISTOLS AT MY BACK!

BUT THERE'S THE DOOR BEHIND YOU WHICH THEY MAY BREAK IN.

AYE, AND THAT IS PART OF YOUR WORK. NO SOONER THE PISTOL'S CHARGED YOU MUST CLIMB UP ONTO YON BED WHERE YOU'RE HANDY AT THE WINDOW, AND IF THEY LIFT A HAND AGAINST THE DOOR, YE'RE TO SHOOT! WHAT ELSE HAVE YE TO GUARD?

THERE'S THE SKY-LIGHT.

IMPATIENT BECAUSE DAVID HAD NOT RETURNED WITH THE PISTOLS, CAPTAIN HOSEASON VENTURED TO THE ROUND-HOUSE.

STAND!

A NAKED SWORD! THIS IS A STRANGE RETURN FOR HOSPITALITY!

DO YE SEE ME? I AM COME OF KINGS. I BEAR A KING'S NAME. MY BADGE IS AN OAK. DO YE SEE MY SWORD? IT HAS SLASHED THE HEADS OFF MORE WHIGS THAN YE HAVE TOES ON YOUR FEET! CALL UP YOUR VERMIN TO YOUR BACK SIR, AND FALL ON!

I'LL MIND THIS, DAVID!

WHILE DEALING OUT CUTLASSES TO HIS CREW, CAPTAIN HOSEASON PROMISED THEM ONE AND ALL A SHARE OF THE STRANGER'S GOLD.

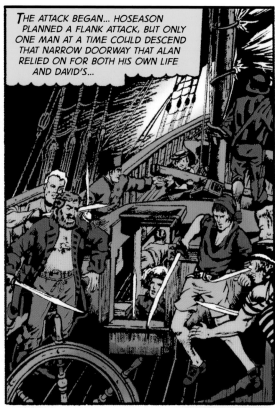

THE ATTACK BEGAN... HOSEASON PLANNED A FLANK ATTACK, BUT ONLY ONE MAN AT A TIME COULD DESCEND THAT NARROW DOORWAY THAT ALAN RELIED ON FOR BOTH HIS OWN LIFE AND DAVID'S...

DAVID, LOOK TO YOUR WINDOW!

THAT I AM!

THERE'S ONE OF YOUR WHIGS FOR YOU!

24

BUT SUDDENLY, THE CREW BROKE OFF TO PLAN A NEW ASSAULT, WHILE BELOW, DAVID WAS HASTILY RECHARGING HIS WEAPONS...

IT WAS SHUAN WHO BUNGLED IT, CAPT'N.

WHEESHT, MAN! HE'S PAID THE PIPER!

FROM THE MUTTERING VOICES OF THE CREW, DAVID COULD SURMISE THAT THEY WERE READY AND ABOUT TO ATTACK AGAIN... IT WAS OF THIS HE WARNED ALAN...

IT'S WHAT WE HAVE TO PRAY FOR! UNLESS WE CAN GIVE THEM A GOOD DISTASTE OF US AND DONE WITH IT, THERE'LL BE NO SLEEP FOR EITHER YOU OR ME. BUT THIS TIME, MIND, THEY'LL BE IN EARNEST!

WHILE OUTSIDE THE ROUND-HOUSE, THE CREW TOOK POSITION... LINING STEALTHILY UP TO THE OPEN ROUND-HOUSE...

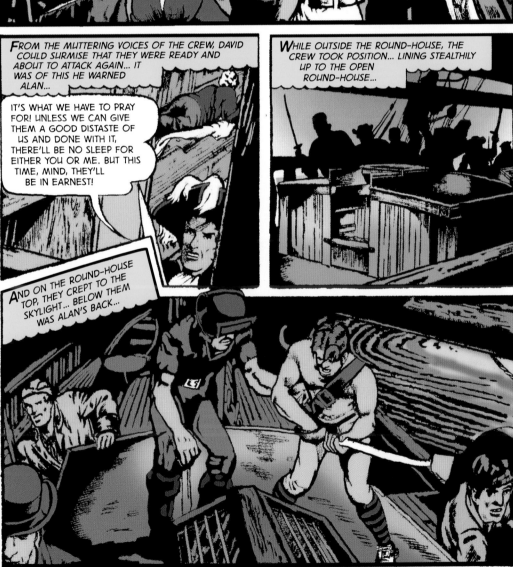

AND ON THE ROUND-HOUSE TOP, THEY CREPT TO THE SKYLIGHT... BELOW THEM WAS ALAN'S BACK...

THEN THERE CAME A SINGLE CALL ON THE SEAPIPE... IT WAS THE SIGNAL...

DAVID HELD OFF HIS SHARE, BUT ALAN WAS SURROUNDED AS WELL AS OUTNUMBERED...

DAVID!

CATCHING UP A CUTLASS, DAVID RUSHED TO HIS FRIEND'S ASSISTANCE...

SUDDENLY, THE ATTACKERS BROKE AND FELL AGAINST ONE ANOTHER IN THEIR HASTE TO LEAVE, WHILE ALAN DROVE THEM ALONG THE DECK AS A SHEEP-DOG DRIVES SHEEP...

AS CAUTIOUS AS HE WAS BRAVE, ALAN RETURNED TO THE ROUND-HOUSE...

DAVID, I LOVE YOU LIKE A BROTHER, AND O, MAN, AM I NO A BONNY FIGHTER!

AFTER PASSING HIS SWORD CLEAN THROUGH EACH OF THE FOUR ENEMIES AND TUMBLING THEM OUT OF DOORS, ALAN BRECK TURNED TO DAVID, MAKING PLANS FOR THE NIGHT...

I'LL TAKE THE FIRST WATCH. YOU'VE DONE WELL BY ME, DAVIE. FIRST AND LAST, I WOULDN'T LOSE YOU FOR ALL APPIN*.

*A PLACE IN SCOTLAND

HOURS PASSED BEFORE DAVID TOOK HIS WATCH.

I'LL WELCOME THE DAYLIGHT...

AND THUS, SUNRISE BROKE OVER SEA AND SHIP...

AT A BREAKFAST OF BREAD AND WINE, ALAN CUT A SILVER BUTTON FROM HIS COAT...

I HAD THESE BUTTONS FROM MY FATHER, DUNCAN STEWART, AND NOW GIVE ONE OF THEM TO YOU AS A KEEPSAKE FOR LAST NIGHT'S WORK. AND WHEREVER YE GO AND SHOW THAT BUTTON, THE FRIENDS OF ALAN BRECK WILL COME AROUND YOU.

Suddenly, Alan and David were hailed by Mr Riach. In the rainfall, David took a strategic position atop the round-house...

THE CAPTAIN WOULD LIKE TO SPEAK WITH YOUR FRIEND. THEY MIGHT SPEAK AT THE WINDOW.

AND HOW DO WE KNOW WHAT TREACHERY IT MEANS?

HE MEANS NONE; AND IF HE DID, I'LL TELL YE THE HONEST TRUTH, WE COULD NOT GET MEN TO FOLLOW.

YE'VE MADE A SORE HASH OF MY BRIG. I HAVEN'T ENOUGH HANDS LEFT TO WORK HER. THERE'S NOTHING LEFT ME BUT TO PUT BACK INTO THE PORT OF GLASGOW.

AYE, UNLESS THERE'S NOBODY SPEAKS ENGLISH IN THAT TOWN, I'LL HAVE A BONNY TALE TO TELL. FIFTEEN TARRY SAILORS ON THE ONE SIDE AND A MAN AND A BOY UPON THE OTHER.

Alan's reply struck home. Captain Hoseason had no wish to be laughed at in Glasgow...

WHERE WE LIE WE ARE BUT A FEW HOURS' SAIL FROM ARDNAMURCHAN*. GIVE ME SIXTY GUINEAS AND I'LL SET YOU THERE.

AM I TO RUN JEOPARDY OF THE REDCOATS? TO PLEASE YOU? NO, SIR, IF YE WANT SIXTY GUINEAS, EARN THEM AND SET ME DOWN WITHIN THIRTY MILES OF MY OWN COUNTRY, EXCEPT IN A COUNTRY OF THE CAMPBELLS.

*IN THE COUNTY OF WEST ARGYLLSHIRE, SCOTLAND

IF I HAD LOST LESS MONEY ON THIS CRUISE, I WOULD SEE YOU IN A ROPE'S END BEFORE I RISKED MY BRIG. BUT THERE'S ONE THING MORE: WE MAY MEET IN WITH A KING'S SHIP AND SHE MAY LAY US ABOARD WITH NO BLAME OF MINE. NOW, IF THAT WAS TO BEFALL, YE MIGHT LEAVE THE MONEY.

CAPTAIN, IF YE SEE A KING'S SHIP, IT SHALL BE YOUR PART TO RUN AWAY!

DAVID AND ALAN EXCHANGED STORIES, DURING WHICH TIME ALAN TOLD OF HIS CHIEF FOE, KNOWN AMONG HIS CLANSMEN AS THE RED FOX... SUDDENLY, THE CAPTAIN INTERRUPTED...

HERE, COME OUT AND SEE IF YOU CAN PILOT!

IS THIS ONE OF YOUR TRICKS?

DO I LOOK LIKE TRICKS? I HAVE OTHER THINGS TO THINK OF! MY BRIG'S IN DANGER!

BY THE CONCERNED LOOK OF HOSEASON'S FACE AND HIS SHARP TONES, IT WAS PLAIN THAT HE WAS EARNEST, SO WITH NO GREAT FEAR OF TREACHERY, DAVID AND ALAN STEPPED ON DECK.

WHAT DO YE CALL THAT?

THE SEA BREAKING ON A REEF, AN' NOW YOU KNOW WHERE IT IS, WHAT BETTER WOULD YE HAVE?

AYE, IF IT WERE THE ONLY ONE. IF I HAD KNOWN OF THESE REEFS, IT IS NOT SIXTY GUINEAS, NO NOR SIX HUNDRED WOULD HAVE MADE ME RISK MY BRIG IN SUCH A STONE-YARD! ARE THERE MANY OF THEM?

TRULY, I AM NO PILOT, BUT THESE'LL BE THE TORRAN ROCKS AND THERE ARE TEN MILES OF THEM.

WE'LL HAVE TO HAUL OUR WIND, MR RIACH. WE'RE IN FOR IT NOW, AND MAY AS WE'LL CRACK ON!

MR RIACH WENT ALOFT...

THE SEA TO THE SOUTH IS THICK REEF TO WINDWARD!

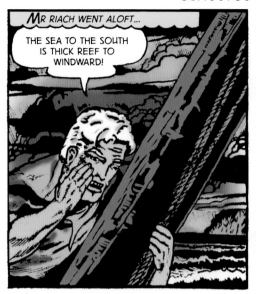

AS HE SPOKE, THE TIDE CAUGHT THE BRIG, SNAPPING THE WIND FROM HER SAIL... SHE CAME ROUND INTO THE WIND LIKE A TOP AND THE NEXT MOMENT, STRUCK A REEF WITH TERRIFIC FORCE.

THE REEF WAS OFF A SMALL ISLE CALLED EARRAID WHICH LAY LOW AND BLACK ON THE LARBOARD*. AS THE SAILORS WORKED AT THE SKIFF, THOSE OF THE WOUNDED WHO COULD HELP CLAMBERED OUT OF THE FORECASTLE. CAPTAIN HOSEASON STOOD HOLDING THE SHROUDS, MUTTERING TO HIMSELF AND GROANING ALOUD WHENEVER THE SHIP HAMMERED THE ROCKS...

WHAT COUNTRY IS THIS?

THE WORST POSSIBLE FOR ME. IT IS A LAND OF THE CAMPBELLS!

A FRIGHTENED SAILOR SHOUTED ABOVE THE TUMULT...

HOLD ON!

*LEFT OR "PORT" SIDE

30

JUST THEN, THE "COVENANT" STRUCK A ROCK AND DAVID WAS HURLED INTO THE SEA, WHERE HE FLOUNDERED HELPLESSLY IN THE SURF...

FINALLY, HE FOUND HIMSELF CLINGING TO A SPAR IN QUIET WATERS.

AFTER AN HOUR OF KICKING AND SPLASHING, HE ARRIVED ON A BARREN, DESERTED BEACH.

AND AT DAYBREAK, THE BOY CLIMBED A HILLTOP FOR A SIGHT OF THE "COVENANT", BUT THE BRIG HAD LIFTED FROM THE REEF AND SUNK... NOR WAS THERE ANY SIGN OF HIS COMPANIONS.

FOUR DAYS AND NIGHTS DAVID WAS MAROONED ON EARRAID BEFORE HE LEARNED IT WAS A TIDAL ISLET AND COULD BE ENTERED OR LEFT FOR THE NEARBY INHABITED ISLE OF MULL TWICE IN EVERY TWENTY-FOUR HOURS. AT MULL, HE LEARNED HIS SHIPMATES WERE SAVED...

WAS THERE ONE DRESSED LIKE A GENTLEMAN?

THE FIRST MAN, THE ONE THAT CAME HERE ALONE, WORE BREECHES AND STOCKINGS, WHILE THE OTHERS HAD SAILOR'S TROUSERS.

YOU MUST BE THE LAD WITH THE SILVER BUTTON?

WHY, YES, I AM!

THE FRIENDLY COTTAGER FED DAVID AND GAVE HIM A BED FOR THE NIGHT. THEN, EARLY THE NEXT MORN...

YOU ARE TO FOLLOW YOUR FRIEND TO HIS COUNTRY BY TOROSAY!

AFTER SEVERAL DAYS OF WALKING, DAVID MET ONE OF ALAN'S CLANSMEN, A FERRYMAN...

I AM SEEKING SOMEBODY AND IT COMES TO MIND THAT YOU WILL HAVE NEWS OF HIM. ALAN BRECK STEWART IS THE NAME.

THE MAN YE ASK FOR IS IN FRANCE.

BUT...

AWEEL! I THINK YE MIGHT HAVE BEGUN WITH THAT END OF THE STICK. I HAVE WORD TO SEE THAT YE COME SAFE.

THE FERRYMAN MADE HASTE TO GIVE DAVID THE ROUTE ALAN LEFT BEHIND...

SPEAK WITH NO ONE AND AVOID THE WHIGS, CAMPBELLS AND RED SOLDIERS. IF YE SEE ANY COMING, LEAVE THE ROAD AND LIE IN THE BUSH.

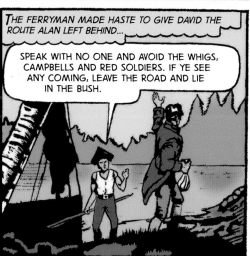

LATER, AS DAVID RESTED, HE WONDERED IN WHICH DIRECTION WAS AUCHARN...

SUDDENLY, THERE WAS THE SOUND OF MEN AND HORSES...

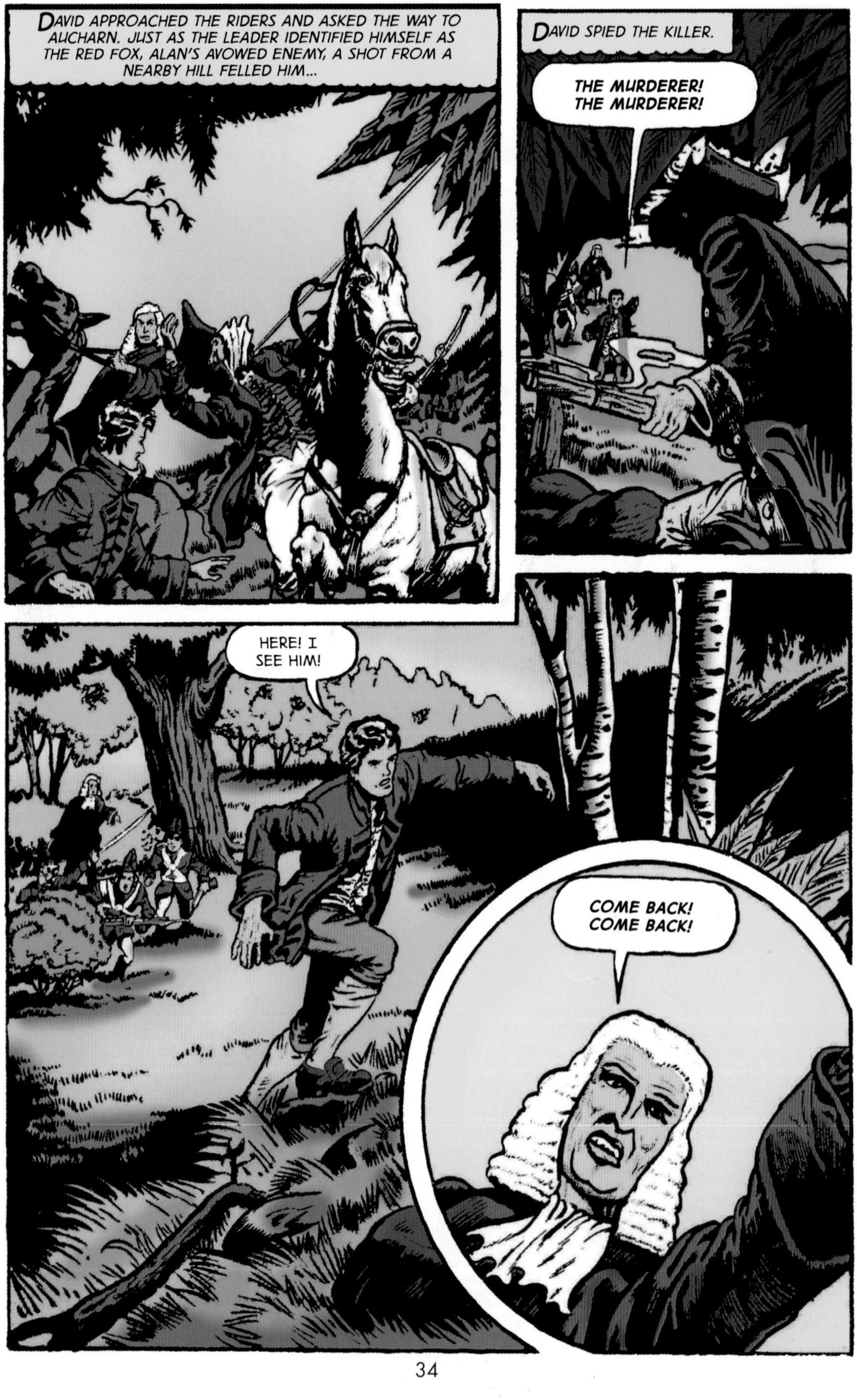
DAVID APPROACHED THE RIDERS AND ASKED THE WAY TO AUCHARN. JUST AS THE LEADER IDENTIFIED HIMSELF AS THE RED FOX, ALAN'S AVOWED ENEMY, A SHOT FROM A NEARBY HILL FELLED HIM...
DAVID SPIED THE KILLER.
THE MURDERER! THE MURDERER!
HERE! I SEE HIM!
COME BACK! COME BACK!

DUCKING THE SHOTS FROM THE SOLDIERS, DAVID RAN INTO THE ARMS OF ALAN.

COME!

YOU!

NOW IT IS EARNEST. DO AS I DO FOR YOUR LIFE!

WITH INFINITE PRECAUTION, ALAN AND DAVID BACKTRACKED ACROSS THE MOUNTAIN TO THE PLACE WHERE THEY HAD MET. THERE, THEY RESTED.

YOU AND I MUST PART, ALAN. I LIKED YOU VERY WELL, BUT YOUR WAYS AREN'T MINE!

I WILL HARDLY PART WITH YE, DAVID, WITHOUT SOME KIND OF REASON.

YE KNOW VERY WELL THAT MAN LYING IN HIS BLOOD ON THE ROAD IS YOUR ENEMY, RED FOX.

I WILL TELL YOU, MR BALFOUR OF SHAWS, IF I WERE GOING TO KILL A GENTLEMAN, IT WOULD NOT BE IN MY OWN COUNTRY TO BRING TROUBLE ON MY CLAN, AND I WOULD NOT GO WANTING SWORD AND GUN, AND WITH A FISHING ROD ON MY BACK!

THAT'S TRUE!

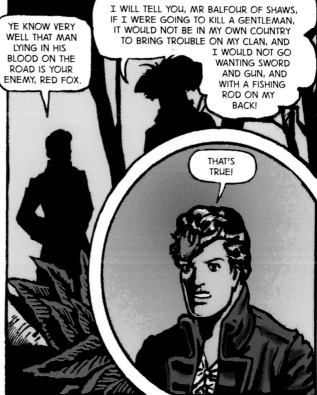

WE'LL STRIKE FOR AUCHARN, THE HOUSE OF MY KINSMAN, WHERE I MUST GET MY CLOTHES AND MY ARMS. THEN, DAVID, WE'LL CRY "FORTH, FORTUNE!" AND TAKE A CAST AMONG THE HEATHER.

ALL THAT DAY, THEY AVOIDED THE SOLDIERS AND BY NIGHT, AUCHARN WAS IN SIGHT...

JAMES MUST HAVE LOST HIS WITS. IF THIS WAS THE SOLDIERS INSTEAD OF YOU AND ME, HE WOULD BE IN A BONNY MESS!

ALAN WHISTLED THREE TIMES, THEN HE AND DAVID WENT DOWN TO MEET JAMES OF THE GLENS.

THIS HAS BEEN A DREADFUL ACCIDENT. IT'LL BRING TROUBLE ON THE COUNTRY.

HOOTS, COLIN ROY IS DEAD, AND BE THANKFUL FOR THAT!

AYE, AND I WISH HE WAS ALIVE AGAIN. IT IS ALL VERY WELL TO BLOW AND BOAST BEFOREHAND, BUT WHO IS TO BEAR THE BLAME OF IT? IT IS APPIN THAT MUST PAY, AND I AM A MAN WITH A FAMILY!

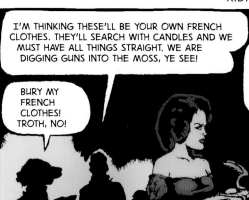

I'M THINKING THESE'LL BE YOUR OWN FRENCH CLOTHES. THEY'LL SEARCH WITH CANDLES AND WE MUST HAVE ALL THINGS STRAIGHT. WE ARE DIGGING GUNS INTO THE MOSS, YE SEE!

BURY MY FRENCH CLOTHES! TROTH, NO!

JAMES OUTFITTED THE FUGITIVES, BUT WARNED...

I'LL HAVE TO OFFER A REWARD FOR YE. IT'S A SORE THING TO DO, BUT IF I GET THE BLAME OF THIS, UNDERSTAND, I'LL HAVE TO FEND FOR MYSELF.

TOMORROW, THERE'LL BE A FINE TO DO IN APPIN, A FINE RIDING OF DRAGOONS AND RUNNING OF REDCOATS. IT BEHOOVES YOU AND ME TO BE GONE.

THE FLIGHT INTO THE HEATHER...

THIS IS NO FIT PLACE FOR YOU AND ME. THIS IS A PLACE THEY'RE BOUND TO WATCH.

A HIDING PLACE...

THE DAY HAS CAUGHT US WHERE WE SHOULD NEVER HAVE BEEN! WE LIE HERE IN SOME DANGER. GO TO YOUR SLEEP, LAD, AND I'LL WATCH.

AFTER THE SOLDIERS HAD SEARCHED THE NEIGHBOURHOOD, ALAN DECIDED ON A DESPERATE COURSE...

COME ALONG, DAVID – AS WELL ONE DEATH AS ANOTHER!

AT SUNDOWN, THE FUGITIVES REACHED A STREAM AND REFRESHED THEMSELVES IN THE COOL WATER.

A WEEK PASSED, BUT DAVID AND ALAN STILL FLED BEFORE THE SEARCHING SOLDIERS...

DO YE SEE YON MOUNTAIN? IF WE CAN WIN TO IT BEFORE MORN WE MAY DO, YET!

BUT ALAN, THAT WILL TAKE US ACROSS THE VERY COMING OF THE SOLDIERS!

DAWN FOUND THEM ON THE MOUNTAIN TOP.

I KNOW THAT, BUT IF WE ARE DRIVEN BACK ON APPIN, WE ARE TWO DEAD MEN! SO NOW, DAVID MAN, BE BRISK!

FINALLY REACHING THE HOME TOWN OF HIS UNCLE, DAVID LEFT ALAN IN HIDING AND SOUGHT MR RANKEILLOR, THE LAWYER...

CAN YOU DIRECT ME, SIR, TO THE HOUSE OF MR RANKEILLOR?

WHY, THAT IS HIS HOUSE I JUST CAME OUT OF, AND FOR A RATHER SINGULAR CHANCE, I AM THAT VERY MAN!

MY NAME IS DAVID BALFOUR.

DAVID BALFOUR? AND WHERE HAVE YOU COME FROM, MR BALFOUR?

I HAVE COME FROM A GREAT MANY PLACES AND I THINK IT WOULD BE WELL TO TELL YOU IN A MORE PRIVATE MANNER.

YES, THAT WILL BE BEST, NO DOUBT.

AT THE END OF DAVID'S STORY...

HAVE YOU ANY PAPERS PROVING YOUR IDENTITY?

NO, SIR, BUT THEY ARE IN THE HANDS OF A MR CAMPBELL, THE MINISTER, AND CAN BE READILY PRODUCED. FOR THAT MATTER, I DO NOT THINK MY UNCLE EBENEZER WOULD DENY ME!

THE LAWYER HEARD A FULL ACCOUNT OF DAVID'S ADVENTURES. HE PRETENDED DEAFNESS AT THE FIRST MENTION OF ALAN BRECK'S NAME, SINCE HE KNEW HIM TO BE A FUGITIVE, AND ASKED DAVID NOT TO USE REAL NAMES IN HIS STORY. HENCE, ALAN BECAME A "MR THOMSON"...

THE ESTATE IS YOURS BEYOND A DOUBT, BUT YOUR UNCLE IS A MAN TO FIGHT. IT'S LIKELY HE'D CALL YOUR IDENTITY IN QUESTION.

THE GREAT AFFAIR IS TO BRING HOME TO HIM THE KIDNAPPING?

SURELY, AND IF POSSIBLE, OUT OF COURT. IF ANY OF YOUR DOINGS WITH YOUR FRIEND WERE TO COME OUT, WE MIGHT FIND THAT WE HAD BURNED OUR FINGERS!

DAVID UNFOLDED A PLAN TO TRAP HIS UNCLE INTO A CONFESSION AND MR RANKEILLOR AGREED TO IT...

TORRANCE, I MUST HAVE THIS WRITTEN OUT FAIR TONIGHT, AND WHEN IT IS DONE, BE READY TO COME ALONG WITH THE GENTLEMAN AND ME.

DRESSED IN NEW CLOTHING PROVIDED BY MR RANKEILLOR, DAVID LED THE WAY TO WHERE HE HAD A RENDEZVOUS WITH ALAN, WHISTLING THE SONG AGREED ON AS A SIGNAL...

MR THOMSON, I HAVE FORGOTTEN MY GLASSES AND OUR FRIEND, DAVID, WILL TELL YOU I'M LITTLE BETTER THAN BLIND AND YOU MUST NOT BE SURPRISED IF I PASS YOU BY TOMORROW!

WHY, SIR, I WOULD SAY IT MATTERS THE LESS AS WE ARE MET HERE FOR A PARTICULAR END, AND BY WHAT I SEE, NOT VERY LIKELY TO HAVE MUCH ELSE IN COMMON.

AT THE SHAW'S, ALAN PUT THEIR PLAN INTO MOTION...

OPEN UP! OPEN UP!

WHAT'S THIS? THIS IS NO TIME OF NIGHT FOR DECENT FOLK AND I HAVE NO DEALING WITH NIGHTHAWKS. WHAT BRINGS YE HERE? I HAVE A BLUNDERBUSS*!

IS THAT YOURSELF, MR BALFOUR? HAVE A CARE WITH THAT BLUNDERBUSS!

*MUZZLE LOADING GUN

WHAT BRINGS ME HERE IS MORE OF YOUR AFFAIR THAN MINE - IT'S DAVID!

DAVID? I'M THINKING I'LL BETTER LET YE IN.

I'M THINKING THAT IT'S HERE UPON THIS DOORSTEP WE MUST CONFER ON THIS BUSINESS. HERE OR NOWHERE, FOR I'M AS STIFF-NECKED AS YOURSELF AND A GENTLEMAN OF A BETTER FAMILY.

YE WILL HAVE HEARD OF THE ISLE OF MULL. IT SEEMS THERE WAS A SHIP LOST IN THOSE PARTS, AND THE NEXT DAY A GENTLEMAN OF MY FAMILY CAME UPON A LAD THAT WAS HALF-DROWNED. HE BROUGHT HIM TO AND CLAPPED HIM IN AN OLD CASTLE, WHERE HE HAS BEEN A GREAT EXPENSE.

ALAN TELLS THE UNCLE THAT UNLESS HE AGREES TO RANSOM DAVID, HE MAY NEVER SEE HIS NEPHEW AGAIN...

I'M NO' VERY CARING. HE WAS NOT A GOOD LAD AND I'VE NO CALL TO INTERFERE.

I SEE WHAT YE WOULD BE AT, PRETENDING YE DON'T CARE... TO MAKE THE RANSOM SMALLER!

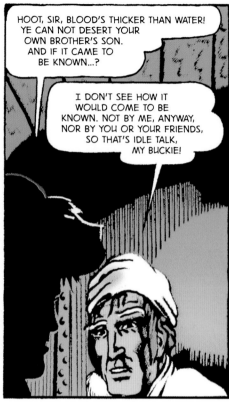

HOOT, SIR, BLOOD'S THICKER THAN WATER! YE CAN NOT DESERT YOUR OWN BROTHER'S SON. AND IF IT CAME TO BE KNOWN...?

I DON'T SEE HOW IT WOULD COME TO BE KNOWN. NOT BY ME, ANYWAY, NOR BY YOU OR YOUR FRIENDS, SO THAT'S IDLE TALK, MY BUCKIE!

THEN IT'LL HAVE TO BE DAVID THAT TELLS IT!

HOW'S THAT?

MY FRIENDS WOULD KEEP YOUR NEPHEW AS LONG AS THERE WAS ANY MONEY TO BE MADE OF IT. BUT IF THERE WAS NONE, THEY WOULD LET HIM GO WHERE HE PLEASED.

AYE! I'LL NOT BE DESIRING THAT, EITHER!

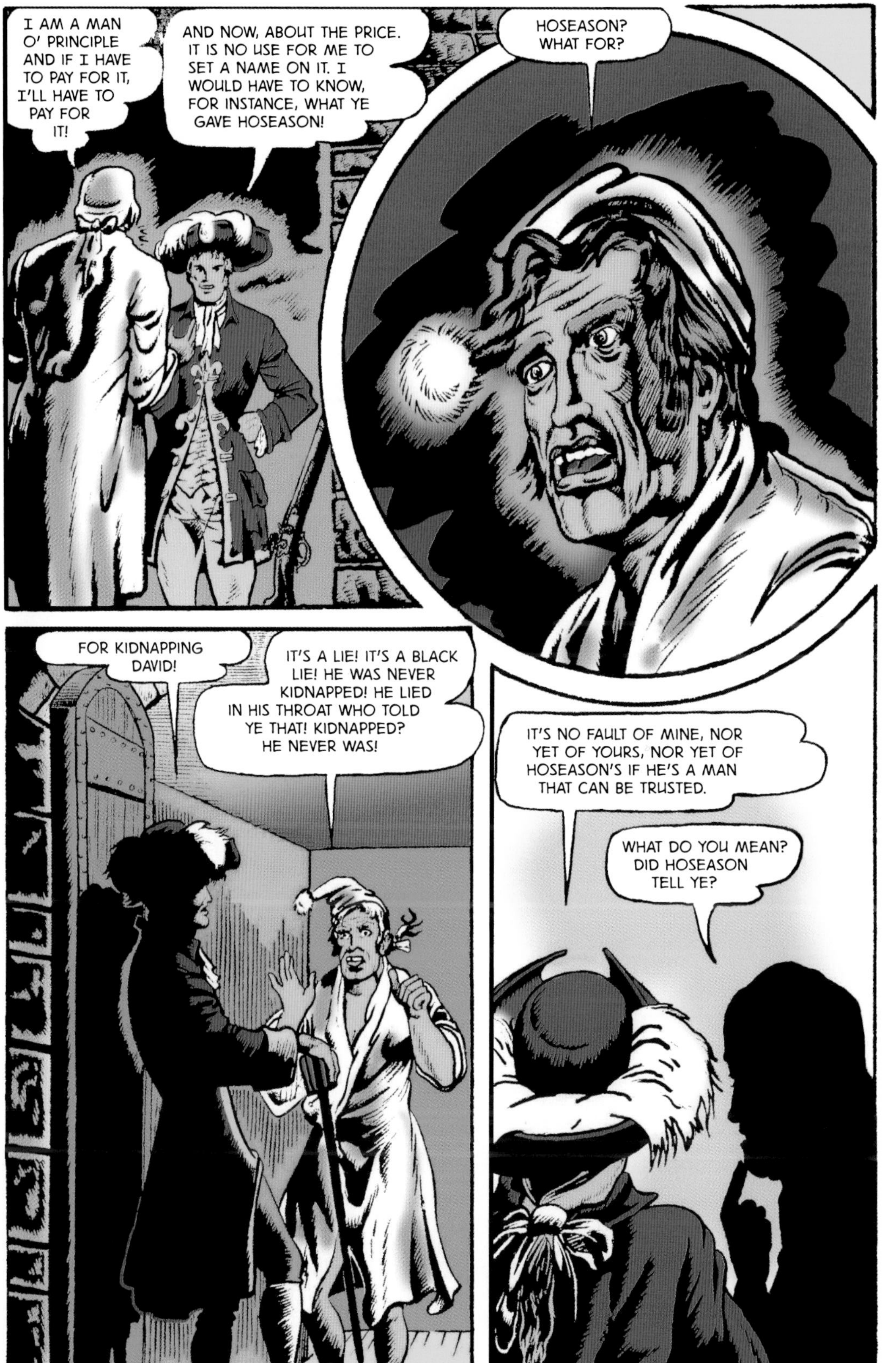
I AM A MAN O' PRINCIPLE AND IF I HAVE TO PAY FOR IT, I'LL HAVE TO PAY FOR IT!
AND NOW, ABOUT THE PRICE. IT IS NO USE FOR ME TO SET A NAME ON IT. I WOULD HAVE TO KNOW, FOR INSTANCE, WHAT YE GAVE HOSEASON!
HOSEASON? WHAT FOR?
FOR KIDNAPPING DAVID!
IT'S A LIE! IT'S A BLACK LIE! HE WAS NEVER KIDNAPPED! HE LIED IN HIS THROAT WHO TOLD YE THAT! KIDNAPPED? HE NEVER WAS!
IT'S NO FAULT OF MINE, NOR YET OF YOURS, NOR YET OF HOSEASON'S IF HE'S A MAN THAT CAN BE TRUSTED.
WHAT DO YOU MEAN? DID HOSEASON TELL YE?

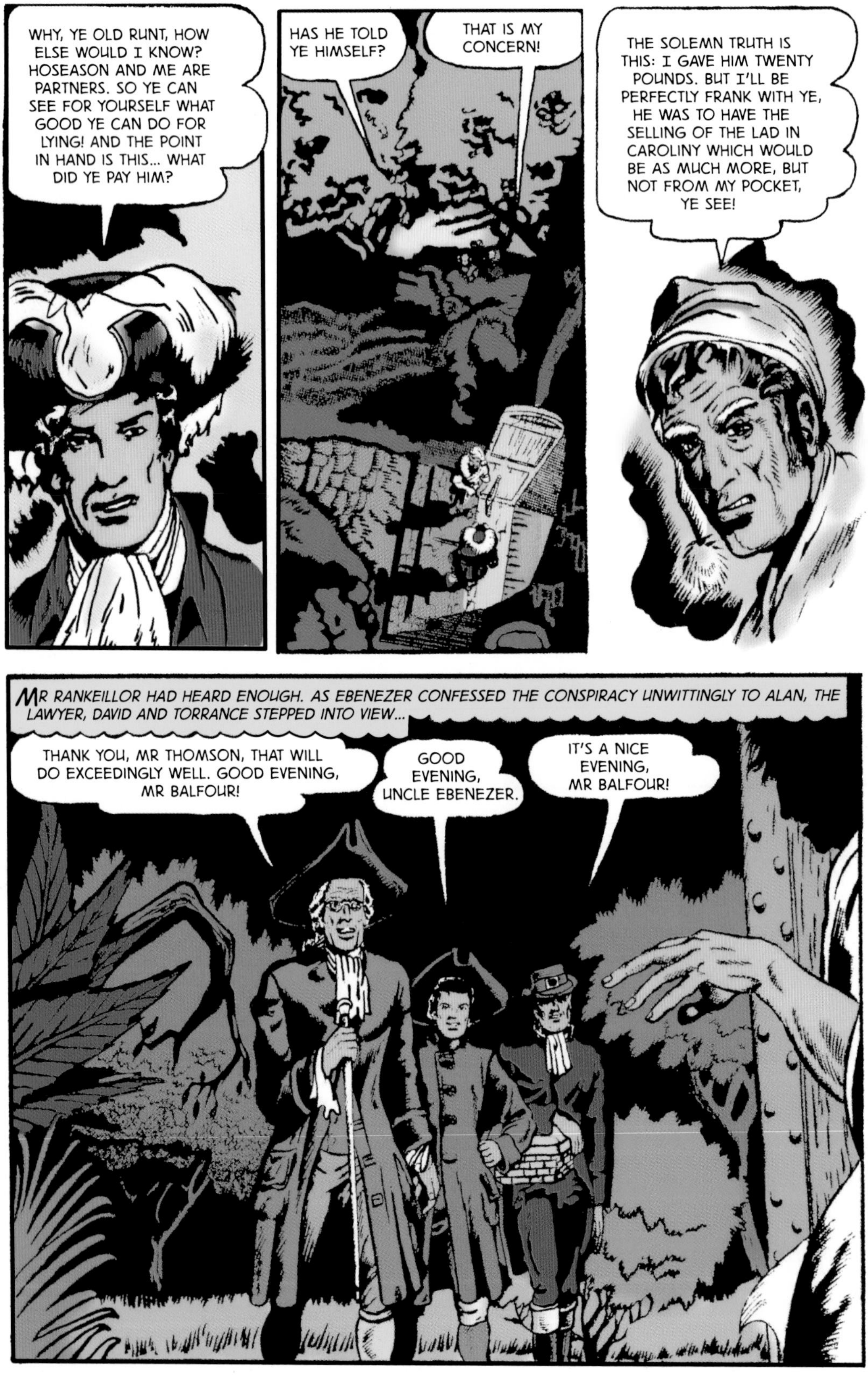
WHY, YE OLD RUNT, HOW ELSE WOULD I KNOW? HOSEASON AND ME ARE PARTNERS. SO YE CAN SEE FOR YOURSELF WHAT GOOD YE CAN DO FOR LYING! AND THE POINT IN HAND IS THIS... WHAT DID YE PAY HIM?
HAS HE TOLD YE HIMSELF?
THAT IS MY CONCERN!
THE SOLEMN TRUTH IS THIS: I GAVE HIM TWENTY POUNDS. BUT I'LL BE PERFECTLY FRANK WITH YE, HE WAS TO HAVE THE SELLING OF THE LAD IN CAROLINY WHICH WOULD BE AS MUCH MORE, BUT NOT FROM MY POCKET, YE SEE!
MR RANKEILLOR HAD HEARD ENOUGH. AS EBENEZER CONFESSED THE CONSPIRACY UNWITTINGLY TO ALAN, THE LAWYER, DAVID AND TORRANCE STEPPED INTO VIEW...
THANK YOU, MR THOMSON, THAT WILL DO EXCEEDINGLY WELL. GOOD EVENING, MR BALFOUR!
GOOD EVENING, UNCLE EBENEZER.
IT'S A NICE EVENING, MR BALFOUR!

EBENEZER WAS STRICKEN DUMB AS HE REALISED HE HAD BEEN TRICKED INTO A CONFESSION BEFORE WITNESSES.

COME, COME, MR EBENEZER. YOU MUST NOT BE DOWNHEARTED. I PROMISE YOU WE SHALL MAKE EASY TERMS.

IN THE MEANTIME, GIVE US THE CELLAR KEY AND TORRANCE SHALL DRAW US A BOTTLE OF WINE IN HONOUR OF THE EVENT.

MR DAVID, I WISH YOU ALL JOY IN YOUR GOOD FORTUNE, WHICH I BELIEVE TO BE DESERVED.

THIS IS TO MY BANKERS, PLACING A CREDIT TO YOUR NAME. I TRUST YOU WILL BE CAREFUL OF YOUR MONEY.

AYE, SIR.

TAKING LEAVE OF MR RANKEILLOR, DAVID AND ALAN WALKED TOWARDS THE CITY OF EDINBURGH. THEY DISCUSSED THEIR PLANS FOR THE FUTURE, BUT EACH WAS THINKING OF THE ADVENTURES THEY SHARED IN THE PAST...

THE FRIENDS AGREED THAT ALAN HAD TO KEEP TO THE COUNTRY UNTIL DAVID SOUGHT OUT A STEWART CLANSMAN WHO WOULD FIND A SHIP FOR ALAN'S ESCAPE FROM SCOTLAND.

WELL, DAVID, MY FRIEND...

GOODBYE, ALAN.

AND THUS, THEY CAME TO THE PARTING OF THE WAYS.

THE END

Robert Louis Stevenson (1850 - 1894)

Excitement filled the little grey house in Edinburgh on the dreary morning of November 13th, 1850, when the first vigorous squalling of Robert Louis Balfour Stevenson filled the sober atmosphere below the ramparts of Edinburgh Castle. Thomas and Margaret Stevenson were delighted with their first (and only) child, and the proud father was already spinning plans to place his son in the family profession of engineering. But the health of junior Stevenson was rather fragile. At eight years, a gastric fever very nearly took him off, and left a weakness which harrassed him during all of his forty-four years.

Stevenson took up engineering, but the tall, extremely thin, dark-haired and restless young man showed signs of more than his chosen cold science. In his first writings, he indicated his future style: this was an anonymous pamphlet called "The Pentland Rising", penned when he was 16. Trying for something less strenuous than engineering, Stevenson studied law and was called before the Edinburgh Bar in 1875.

Stevenson now undertook a period of hard work to groom himself as a writer. With pen constantly in hand, he visited France for the first time in 1875, and a winter at Mentone on the Riviera helped his frail health. When he was outdoors, his health was always better, though his life was a constant series of repairs and relapses. But with every decline in his wellbeing his mind seemed to move ahead to greater strength. His infectious gaiety, originality of thought and kindly, generous disposition, no less than his high courage, won for Stevenson a host of close and devoted friends.

On a return visit to France the following year, he met an American widow, Mrs Osborne, who later became his wife.

His health was again in an alarming state, but he continued to write, and a collection of his essays was published, together with articles, poems and his first romance, *The Sea Cook*, now known the world over as *Treasure Island*. *The New Arabian Nights* was printed in 1882. He kept writing, until *The Strange Case of Dr Jekyll and Mr Hyde* became a widely read favourite. This was followed by another immediately popular book, *Kidnapped*.

However, in 1887, he, his wife and step-son left for the United States, where he spent the first winter at Saranac Lake. In this quiet retreat, the ailing Scottish author wrote most of *The Master of Ballantrae* and many of his finer essays. Moving on to the Pacific Coast, he set sail for the South Pacific in June 1888. The cruise, intended solely for pleasure, turned into a voluntary exile prolonged until the hour of Stevenson's death. The party visited Samoa, and then went on to Australia. He soon returned to Samoa where the last four years of his unquiet life were spent. His health improved enormously there, and he never felt better than he did in his wooden box of a house perched above the blue waters of the Pacific.

On December 3rd, 1894, Robert Louis Stevenson was gaily talking with friends on the verandah of his house when he was struck down by a stroke of apoplexy. He never regained consciousness, and died that evening as the swift tropical dusk closed down on his well-loved eyrie. The next day, sixty of his beloved Samoan neighbours, the natives who called him "Chief," carried the wasted body to the summit of the high peak of Vasa. There, his body is buried, as was his wish, the soft and gently rolling Pacific at his feet, the vaporous puffball clouds canopying his tombstone.

Themes

Kidnapped has just one significant theme. Readers often look at the book as a metaphorical, if highly romantic, representation of Scottish history. The Balfour twins are like England and Scotland, two halves of the same island. Their long-standing battles end with Ebenezer (England) the victor in terms of wealth, but Alexander (the name of the first Scottish King) the winner of happiness. Therefore, David Balfour is the son of Scotland. After the death of Alexander (the end of Scottish independence in 1707), he approaches his uncle for his rightful share of the family resources. He's treated with contempt, nearly killed and at last shanghaied aboard the *Covenant*. The original Scottish *Covenant* was a commitment to religious freedom, but it was clearly more of a political document. Adherence to the path of independence via the *Covenant* leads David into his meeting Alan Breck Stewart. The failed rebellion of 1745 was to back a Stewart as the rightful heir to both the British and the non-existent Scottish thrones. David's experience of being hounded through the very heart of his country for a crime he didn't commit is akin to the experience of many Scots after 1745, a great wrong which could only be rectified by reclaiming a share of the British inheritance and an admission of guilt on the part of the English, or Ebenezer, whichever comes first.

But the problems of political integrity embodied in *Kidnapped* aren't quite as simple as this metaphor might lead a reader to believe. It is very clear, for example, that David and Alan do not represent the same political perspective, even at the end of the novel. David never renounces his faith in the British crown; Alan never relaxes his fidelity to his Scottish lord. These two positions are mutually exclusive, however, because any gain in the clan leaders' power is a direct loss of power for the King of England. This is true not only in the novel, but in history as well. Robert Louis Stevenson has to set the novel in 1751, six years after the defeat of the clan lords, because no one would pay double rent for long. It was soon obvious to even the most remote Highlander that the old ways were gone forever. The rebellion which Alan Breck Stewart represents was plainly dead, and no amount of swashbuckling could bring it back.

Underlying the failure of Alan's dream, however, is the dream itself. What right does England have to outlaw the clans? What authority did the British crown have for claiming rents on lands belonging to the traditional family lords? The situation of aggressive domination has existed since the first family decided it preferred another family's cave to its own. It certainly formed the backbone of settlement in the United States, in which European immigrants to the New World simply disregarded all the prior rights of Native Americans and claimed land - and the right to govern it - for themselves. The colonists' descendants tried to make up for these actions, which are generally judged as amoral, by giving native tribes large blocks of land which they are free to run almost as independent countries - but even the establishment of these reservations is fraught with difficulties. What if a drill sunk outside a reservation sucks up oil from under a reservation? Who gets the money? This type of problem is even more severe in places like Liberia, Somalia and many of the former republics of the USSR. Where does traditional authority begin and the asserted rule of law end? *Cont'd*

In *Kidnapped*, David is confronted with this problem when he first arrives at the Shaws. His uncle locks him in the room. He is no better than a prisoner, whatever his rightful relationship with the Balfour fortune. Ebenezer has the gun and Ebenezer has the keys; thus Ebenezer has the power. David manages to temporarily reverse the power structure (he soon locks up his uncle) but his uncle's treachery undermines David's efforts at negotiating a fair settlement. Once on board the *Covenant*, the problem of power again resurfaces. Who has the authority over the ship? At first, there is no question, and if Captain Hoseason hadn't blundered in trusting David there never would have been. Even after the battle of the round-house, the balance of power proves impossible to maintain. Throughout their escape, David and Alan struggle to achieve a kind of balance, too, and they never do, although they do gain one another's respect. Is that the best a Government can do with a rebellious population: respect a gang's right to run its own property? What happens when a gang begins to demand tribute - in the form of rent or taxes - from the people on its own land? There are few good solutions to this problem. Robert Louis Stevenson was wise enough to leave the matter unresolved at the end of *Kidnapped*. But how could people do better in circumstances where an advanced civilisation encroaches into the territory of a less advanced people? And then consider the ultimate question - how would earth fare if advanced civilisations - aliens - visited us and began to covet our caves, and that they had the power to implement those desires? A fascinating question - but not a new one!

———————∞———————

Scotland

When you look at a map of the world, Great Britain appears to be a single entity, one nation, undivided. In recent years, the name Great Britain has given way to the term United Kingdom, but while control of Scotland, Northern Ireland and Wales is now accepted within the United Kingdom, control in Ireland has been fraught with centuries of long strife and control in Scotland was uncertain until midway through the eighteenth century. While the Scottish cities and coastline were firmly under English domination in 1751, when *Kidnapped* takes place, and had been for at least a hundred years and politically since 1707, a different system ruled in the remote Scottish Highlands. For a thousand years or more, the people of Scotland had organised themselves by family alliance. These clans, each one signified by costumes made of an emblematic plaid called a tartan, were the government. For the most part, the families took care of their own land and their own business as they saw fit and the clan leader was the accepted King of any territory belonging to a member of the tribe. Whenever something needed doing that was larger than one clan could cope with - such as fighting against an outside invader, most likely from England - clan leaders met and formulated plans together, sometimes working with whoever sat on the Scottish throne, but just as frequently were in conflict with both the King and each other. Through tentative agreements, intermarriage and violence over succession to clan leadership, the network governing Scotland had become a tangled web no-one but a Scotsman could understand. The differences both within Scotland and between ***Cont'd***

Scotland and England were also religious and bitter disagreements between English Anglican and Scotch Presbyterians fuelled an ongoing war. The 1688 Scottish *Covenant* - like the ship on which David Balfour is kidnapped - was a declaration of Scottish independence, both political and religious.

Even after Britain claimed the unity of Scotland and England in 1707, the King of England cared a great deal about this separate government in the Scottish Highlands because these Scots owed money to the crown. Also, with the English getting set to fight a war in France and to police America and Ireland, the royal authority wanted both to have enough soldiers on hand and to prevent the rebellious Highlanders from becoming enemy spies; after all, they had no allegiance to the King, which they had proved in a disastrous rebellion in 1745. To most people in Great Britain - even the urban Scots - the Highland clans were not much different from gangs of outlaws - like Italian crime families in 20th century America, only with history on their side. Despite the defeat of the Highland rebels and the enforcement of laws banning every vestige of the clan system, the crown had difficulty subduing a place fraught with such uncertain alliances.

Alan Breck Stewart sides firmly with the Scottish clans. David Balfour believes in the British crown. They are a historically unlikely duo, emblematic of peace in a world of shifting national boundaries.

Key Characters

David Balfour: The teenage orphan of a small-town Scottish schoolmaster and his beloved wife.

Ebenezer Balfour: David's long-lost uncle, a loner and a miser who jealously guards the family fortune.

Mr Rankeillor: Ebenezer Balfour's lawyer.

Captain Hoseason: Co-owner, with Ebenezer Balfour, of the *Covenant*.

Mr Shuan: First mate on the *Covenant* and its navigator.

Mr Riach: The *Covenant*'s second mate, friendly to David.

Alan Breck Stewart: A warrior and agent for the rebel Scottish Highlanders.

Colin Campbell of Glenure: King George's agent, known to his enemies as "the Red Fox".

Torrance: Rankeillor's trusted assistant.

Discussion Topics

1) Who are the Stewarts, from whom Alan claims his royal lineage? How important is a knowledge of Scottish history in understanding the novel?

2) Women are very scarce in *Kidnapped*. Why does Stevenson avoid women in the book? Does the absence of female characters indicate that the book is not for female readers? Do you think men and women, or boys and girls, will get something different from the novel?

3) One can frequently discover what a novelist regards as the most important event of a book by looking at the pages which occupy the middle. In *Kidnapped*, the event at the centre is the assassination of Colin Campbell, the Red Fox. Why would Stevenson place that murder at the middle of the book?

4) Stevenson's relationship with his father was strained, frequently to the point of breaking, and *Kidnapped* can be read as his working out his hostility towards Thomas Stevenson. Although David's father has died before the novel itself begins, he still conducts a number of father-son relationships. Which relationships fit into this category and how do they lead to a resolution?

5) Captain Hoseason appears to be entirely without morals. Is he? He certainly sees money as having a high moral value. He is offended by Alan Breck Stewart's traitorous wearing of a French army uniform. Given all these aspects of his character, how would you describe Hoseason's morality?

6) Compare David Balfour and Alan Breck Stewart. Who would you rather call a friend? Who do you admire more? Why?

Timeline

1875 - The United States Congress passes the Civil Rights Act, which prohibits racial discrimination in public accommodations and jury duty.

Jeanne Calment is born and would eventually become the longest-living human being in recorded history. She lived until 1997, at the age of 122 years, 164 days.

1876 - Alexander Graham Bell is granted a patent for an invention he calls the telephone.

1877 - The phonograph is invented by Thomas Edison.

1884 - The first edition of the *Oxford English Dictionary* is published.

1886 - Karl Benz is awarded the patent for his invention of the first motor car.

***Kidnapped* first published.**

1887 - The British Empire celebrates Queen Victoria's Golden Jubilee, marking the 50th year of her reign.

1889 - The Eiffel Tower opens in Paris.

1892 - Sir Arthur Conan Doyle publishes *The Adventures of Sherlock Holmes*.

1893 - *Catriona*, also known as *David Balfour*, a sequel to *Kidnapped*, telling of Balfour's further adventures, is published.

Gandhi commits his first act of civil disobedience in India.